A GUESSING-GAME STORY

Bear Goes Shopping

by Harriet Ziefert
pictures by Arnold Lobel

Sterling Publishing Co., Inc.
New York

Bear likes to shop a little every day.
What does he buy? See if you can guess.

It's Monday. Bear is going to the bakery.
What will he buy? See if you can guess.

It's Tuesday. Bear is going to the pet store.
What will he buy? See if you can guess.

It's Wednesday. Bear is going to the grocery. What will he buy? See if you can guess.

It's Thursday. Bear is going to the bookstore.
What will he buy? See if you can guess.

It's Friday. Bear is going to the hardware store. What will he buy? See if you can guess.

On Saturday Bear works in the yard.

And on Sunday he rests.
Take it easy, Bear.